Daisy Dawson

Is on Her Way!

Daisy Dawson
Is on Her Way!

Steve Voake
illustrated by Jessica Meserve

SCHOLASTIC INC.
New York Toronto London Auckland Sydney
Mexico City New Delhi Hong Kong Buenos Aires

ISBN-13: 978-0-545-11020-4
ISBN-10: 0-545-11020-3

12 11 10 9 8 7 6 5 4 3 2 1   8 9 10 11 12 13/0

Printed in the U.S.A.   40

First Scholastic printing, September 2008

This book was typeset in StempelSchneidler.
The illustrations were done in ink and pencil.

For Jon Voake, savior of bees
S. V.

To Isabelle:
May magical butterflies kiss your cheeks.
Aunty Jess

Contents

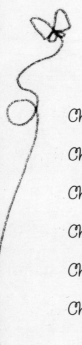

Chapter 1   An Unusual Conversation   1

Chapter 2   Cheesy Cheddars   15

Chapter 3   Ant Music   31

Chapter 4   Sky-Flowers   49

Chapter 5   Mission Impossible   59

Chapter 6   Daisy's Magic   87

Chapter 1

An Unusual Conversation

"Daisy, don't dawdle!" called her mother as Daisy Dawson ambled out into the sunshine and stopped to pick up a worm that was stranded on the path. "Miss Frink said you were late three times last week!"

Daisy smiled to herself as the worm wriggled in her hand.

Late three times.

That meant she had actually been on time twice.

Not too bad.

She tipped the worm into the flower bed and watched it burrow through the crumbly earth. Then she stood up, hitched her backpack over her shoulder, and skipped down the garden path.

"Don't worry, Mom," she said, dusting her hands together and swinging around the gatepost. "Daisy Dawson is on her way!"

The day was warm, and the sky was china blue. Bees buzzed among the foxgloves, and Daisy wandered down the lane, humming a little tune to herself.

Suddenly, from the corner of her eye, she caught sight of a beautiful yellow butterfly stuck in a spider's web. As she crouched down to take a closer look, a black spider emerged from beneath a leaf and began crawling across the web toward it.

"Oh, no, you don't!" said Daisy,
cupping her hand protectively
around the struggling insect. As the
spider scuttled back to its hiding
place, Daisy scooped the butterfly
out of the web and carefully pulled
some sticky strands from its wings.

"There you go," she said. "Back in the
world again."

Then she smiled and opened her palms
toward the sky.

The butterfly was still for a few moments. Then, very slowly, it spread its wings and fluttered gracefully up into the air. Daisy shielded her eyes against the sun and blinked as the butterfly swooped low past her face, brushing her cheek gently with the tip of its wing. Then it rose once more into the warm air and flew high into the treetops, growing smaller and smaller until finally it was lost from sight.

As Daisy watched it fly away, her cheek began to tingle as though something was sparkling beneath her skin. She touched a hand to her face, and a delicious warm feeling fizzed along her fingers, tumbling like a wave through

her whole
body until it reached all the way
down to the tips of her toes.

"That's strange," she whispered.

Just then, somewhere among the white
blossoms of an apple tree, a blackbird began
to sing. Its sweet music floated down
through the spring sky and, to her
astonishment, Daisy realized that she could
understand exactly what the blackbird was
singing about. The notes spun softly around
her like strands of silk, weaving a song about
clouds and apples, sunshine and stars.

Daisy gasped in surprise and shook her
head.

"Now don't be *silly,* Daisy," she told
herself. "Pull yourself together. Birds can't
talk."

It was then that she remembered where
she was supposed to be. Only yesterday,

Miss Frink had told her not to be late again.

Pulling up her backpack, she twirled around and wandered slowly onward toward school. Across the meadow, she could see the white mare tugging at tufts of grass in the shade of the beech tree. Daisy leaned on the gate and peered into the shadows of the tumbledown barn, trying to see if the old stray dog was around. She liked to share a bit of her lunch with him on the way to school. Ham sandwiches were his favorite, and she had made an extra one just in case.

"Rover?" she called, opening up her lunch box. "Rover, come and see what I've got for you!"

A large, grumpy-looking bloodhound stuck his head through a hole in the bricks, blinking and sneezing in the bright sunlight.

His fur was the color of sandstone, and his serious brown eyes stared out from folds of baggy skin that hung down around his face. As he padded toward her, his long floppy ears swung back and forth, flapping up dust from the dry ground.

When he reached the gate, he stopped and looked at her expectantly.

"Good morning," he said in a deep, gravelly voice. "What's on the menu today?"

Daisy was so shocked that she dropped her lunch box and put a hand up to her mouth.

This cannot be happening, she thought. She shut her eyes tightly for a moment or two, then opened them again.

The dog was still there, looking straight at her.

"Ex-excuse me," Daisy said uncertainly, still unable to believe her ears, "but did you say something to me?"

"Of course," replied the dog. "It would have been rude not to." He paused for a moment as if deep in thought, then said slowly, "Wait a minute. . . . Do you actually understand what I'm saying to you?"

"Yes," replied Daisy. "I think I do."

The dog made a noise somewhere between a bark and a laugh.

"This," he said, "is amazing!"

"But you understand me as well," said Daisy. "So that's pretty amazing too."

The dog cocked his head to one side.

"Dogs always understand what humans say," he replied.

"No, they don't," said Daisy. "Take my aunt Kathy's dog. He never does anything she tells him."

The dog's brow crinkled like a little plowed field.

"That doesn't mean he doesn't *understand* her," he said. "He probably just doesn't want to do it."

"Oh," said Daisy thoughtfully. "I see what you mean."

"There you go, then," said the dog.

There was silence for a moment while the two of them thought about this. Then the dog said, "My name's not Rover, by the way. It's Boom." Seeing the puzzled look on

Daisy's face, he added, "I was born on the Fourth of July, you see."

"Really?" Daisy said, smiling. "That must have been a shock for you."

"It was," agreed Boom. "The first things I saw when I opened my eyes were a thousand fireworks exploding above me. Huge blazing stars of red, green, orange, and gold. My mother said it was the whole world celebrating my birthday."

Daisy heard the sadness in Boom's voice and guessed that he probably didn't see his mother anymore.

"Boom's a nice name," she said. "It suits you."

"Thank you," said Boom. "What about you? Do you have a name?"

"Two, actually," said Daisy. "I'm Daisy Dawson."

"Well, Daisy Dawson," said Boom, "I'm pleased to make your acquaintance at last."

"Likewise," said Daisy, and she stuck her arm through the gate.

Boom put his soft paw into her hand. As Daisy shook it, he asked, "Am I the first dog you've ever spoken to?"

"Not exactly," said Daisy. "I mean, I've spoken to lots of dogs before. But you're the first one who's ever replied."

Boom chuckled. "Well, imagine that," he said. Then he licked his lips and peered longingly through the gate at Daisy's fallen lunch box.

"I don't suppose you've got any spare food in there?"

"Of course," said Daisy, picking up the lunch box. "Actually, I've brought along your favorite."

Boom raised an eyebrow.

"Not *ham*?" he asked.

"Honey-roasted," said Daisy, producing a sandwich with a flourish. "Extra thick."

"You," said Boom, "are an angel from heaven."

Daisy giggled. "Tell that to Miss Frink."

Then she looked at her watch and remembered.

"Oh, my goodness," she exclaimed. "I'm going to be late for school!"

"Is that bad?" asked Boom through a mouthful of sandwich.

"Miss Frink thinks so," said Daisy.

She turned to go, then looked back over her shoulder and waved. "Nice talking to you, Boom," she called. "See you again soon."

Then, hitching up her backpack, she ran down the dusty lane toward the gates of Nettlegreen Elementary School.

Chapter 2
Cheesy Cheddars

"What was it this time?" asked Miss Frink as Daisy tiptoed into the classroom and mouthed, *Sorry I'm late!* over the top of Marty Johnson's head. "A tornado, perhaps? An avalanche? An earthquake in the lane?"

As the rest of the class giggled into their reading books, Daisy shook her head and slid into her seat. "No, Miss Frink," she said. "It was none of those things."

"Really?" replied the teacher icily. "Well, Daisy, you surprise me."

Daisy took out
her pink pencil case and hooked her
backpack over her chair, hoping she
might get off lightly this time. But
Miss Frink was obviously in the mood for
some entertainment.

"Perhaps, then, Miss Dawson, you would
like to tell us all exactly why you *are* late
again today."

Daisy hesitated. She was an honest girl,
and it was not in her nature to tell a lie. But
she realized that "I've been talking to a dog"
was unlikely to go over well with Miss Frink.

So she said, "I'm afraid I completely forgot what the time was, Miss Frink."

Which was true, of course. It just left out the interesting parts.

"*Again?*" said Miss Frink.

"Sorry," said Daisy. "I'll try to be on time tomorrow."

"Trying is not good enough," said Miss Frink. "You *will* be on time tomorrow." She snapped the attendance book shut and peered at Daisy over the top of her glasses. "*Won't* you, Daisy?"

"Yes, Miss Frink," said Daisy. "I promise."

At that moment, Bobby Mitchell fell backward off his chair and everyone was told to Stop Laughing Because It Wasn't Funny and He Could Have Been Killed.

The long, hot morning wore on.

Daisy was soon so busy trying to work out whether 121 ÷ 7 had a remainder (and if so, what to do with it) that she forgot about her strange conversation with Boom. She had just discovered that the remainder was 2 when she heard a small, squeaky voice say:

"Oh, *wow*. Cheesy Cheddars!"

Daisy looked around to see if anyone else had heard it, but Miss Frink was in the corner explaining hundreds, tens, and ones to the Orange Group, and the rest of the class had their heads down over their math books.

"I *love* Cheesy Cheddars."

"Hang on, Burb—don't eat 'em all! I'm coming over!"

Glancing into the corridor, Daisy saw a small gerbil scampering beneath the row of coats. It stopped for a second, sniffed the air, and then disappeared into a lunch box

that had fallen open on the floor.

There was the sound of giggling, followed by crunching noises.

"These are great, aren't they?" said a little voice happily.

"Cheesy Cheddars are my number one favorite," said the other voice. "They taste like the sun just blew up in your mouth."

"*Bam!*" exclaimed the first voice. "Deeelicious!" This was followed by a lot more giggling.

Daisy suddenly remembered that Bobby Mitchell had been playing with the class gerbils—Burble and Furball—earlier that morning. She looked anxiously across at the glass tank full of straw and sawdust and noticed that the top had not been put back on properly. A half-chewed cardboard toilet-paper tube was pushed up against the side of the tank.

Burble and Furball were nowhere to be seen.

Uh-oh, thought Daisy.

Placing her pencil neatly along the crease of her math book, she thrust her hand up into the air.

"I don't care who started it," Miss Frink was saying to Wayne Bishop. "I'm telling you to stop it right now!"

Daisy coughed politely.

"Excuse me," she said.

"Yes, Daisy?" said Miss Frink impatiently. "What is it?"

"We haven't taken the attendance book up to the office yet." Daisy smiled her biggest, most helpful smile. "Should I take it up for you?"

Miss Frink frowned.

"Have you finished your math yet?"

Daisy looked down at her book.

"Almost," she said. "I'm on the problems now."

You can say that again, she thought to herself.

"Well," said Miss Frink, softening a little, "that would be very helpful, Daisy. But don't be long. And don't dawdle!"

"I won't," said Daisy, picking up the attendance book from Miss Frink's desk.

She closed the classroom door behind her and stood next to the coats, listening carefully.

"What's your favorite?" asked a small voice. "Sunflower seeds or sandwiches?"

"Dunno," replied another little voice. "I've never had a sandwich." There was a pause. "When have you ever had a sandwich?"

"Well," said the first voice, sounding as if its mouth were full of something, "actually, I'm having one *right now*!"

This was followed by a joyful cry of "Oh, it's a *cheesy* sandwich!" and the sound of little voices giggling with their mouths full.

Daisy crouched down next to the coats.

"Excuse me," she said, "but I think that's someone else's lunch you're eating."

The giggling stopped.

"Did you hear that?" a voice whispered.

"Yes, I did," whispered the other. "Was she talking to us?"

"Don't be silly," said the first voice. "Since when have kids been able to talk to gerbils?"

"Actually, I *am* talking to you," announced Daisy. "And what's more, I know you can hear me."

There was a spluttering noise and the sound of cheesy breadcrumbs being sprayed around the lunch box. Then a furry little face poked out from under the plastic cover. When it saw Daisy, it whipped back inside.

"It's a girl!" it squeaked. "And she *is* talking to us!"

"You're pulling my leg," said the first voice.

"If you don't believe me, take a look for yourself. Go on!"

Another tiny face appeared and stared at Daisy, its shiny brown eyes widening with surprise. Then it shot back inside and banged its head on the lid.

"*Ow–chee!*"

"See? Told you."

"Listen," said Daisy patiently. "I'm not

going to hurt you. I just want a word with you, that's all."

There was a rustling sound and the two gerbils popped their heads out of the lunch box.

"You're a talking girl!" said one. Daisy recognized him as Furball by the little white patch on his nose. "How amazing is that?"

"Not as amazing as my first-ever cheesy sandwich," said Burble. She slid back into the lunch box and let out a tiny burp. "Oopsy, excuse me."

"You really shouldn't be out here," said Daisy. "Miss Frink will be very upset if she finds out you've run away."

"Well," replied Burble, "in that case, she should give us cheesy sandwiches, shouldn't she?"

"Cheese sandwiches aren't proper food for gerbils," said Daisy. "If you had them all the time, you'd probably get sick."

"It'd be worth it," said Furball. "They're *fantastic*!"

"Listen," said Daisy, trying to get the conversation back on track. "I really think you should go back to your tank now."

"Don't want to," said Furball. "The food's boring and it's got sawdust in it."

"That's 'cause you keep throwing it on the floor," said Burble. "If you ate it out of the dish, there'd be no problem."

"Ooh, listen to her," said Furball, putting on a snooty voice. *"'That's because you keep throwing it on the floor. . . .'"* I throw it on the floor because it's so *boring*. I want Cheesy Cheddars, thank you very much."

"Tell you what," said Daisy. "If you go back to your tank now, I'll give you both a Cheesy Whatsit from my lunch box when I get back."

"Oooh," said Furball, sounding interested. "What's a Whatsit?"

"I know—I know—I know—I know!" squealed Burble excitedly. "They're those

26

orange things that go *crunch—crunch—crunch* and then afterward everything tastes of cheese. Even the air in your nose!"

"Whoa," said Furball. "I have *got* to get me one of those."

"So we've got ourselves a deal, then?" asked Daisy.

"Make it two," said Burble.

"Two what?" said Daisy.

"Two Whatsits each, and you're on."

Daisy looked doubtful. "I don't want you to be sick," she said. "Two Whatsits seems like an awful lot for one gerbil."

"We could save one for later," suggested Furball.

"Yeah *right,*" said Burble. "That is *so* going to happen. But come on, two Whatsits won't kill us. What d'you say?"

Daisy nodded, then took one paw from each gerbil gently between her finger and thumb and shook them.

"OK," she said. "Deal." Then, watching them scamper off toward the classroom, she remembered the attendance book and quickly made her way to the office.

As soon as school was over, Daisy grabbed her backpack and ran up the lane as fast as her legs would carry her. She could hardly wait to see Boom again, to tell him about the gerbils, and ask him if there was anything special he wanted on his sandwich tomorrow.

But when she leaned over the gate and called to him, there was no response.

Daisy was puzzled. Where was he? Boom always wandered out to see her when she called. Clambering over the fence into the field, she made her way across to the old barn and peered through the broken window.

Apart from some straw and a rusty tractor, the barn was empty.

Boom was nowhere to be seen.

Chapter 3
Ant Music

The next morning, Daisy woke up feeling sure
that Boom would be back in his usual place.
He had probably just gone out for a walk,
she thought. She decided to make him a treat
and was just putting an extra-thick ham and
ketchup sandwich into her lunch box when
her dad came past on his way out to work.

"You must have hollow legs, Daisy," he
said, taking a quick swig of coffee and
ruffling her hair. "You've got enough in there
to feed an army!"

"She's a growing girl," said Mom. "Aren't you, my love?"

"Hope so," said Daisy, who was still one of the smallest in her class.

"Now then," said Dad, kissing her on the top of her head. "Didn't I ever tell you that the best things come in small packages?"

Walking along the path next to the meadow, Daisy stopped and leaned over the gate.

"Boom!" she called softly. "I've made your favorite sandwich!"

But there was still no sign of him.

And as Daisy listened, the only sound was the wind whispering softly past the stones and the grass and the broken window.

Miss Frink was so amazed to see Daisy arrive on time for once that she gave her a yellow smiley sticker and sent her up to the office with the attendance book. The secretary

was busy, so Daisy
sat on a chair in the
corridor and thought
about all the unusual
things that had been
happening. And the
more she thought
about them, the more
ridiculous they seemed.

A talking dog named
Boom? Gerbils discussing cheesy snacks?
Swinging her feet above the polished wooden
floor, Daisy watched specks of dust dancing
in a shaft of sunlight and decided that it
was probably time to stop daydreaming
and join the real world. Wasn't that what
people were always telling her? Maybe the
sooner she forgot about the whole thing,
the better.

But even if Boom couldn't talk, she was
still worried about him. Where had he gone?

Daisy's thoughts were interrupted by a tiny sound, like someone singing a long way off.

"Dubbedy dum-dum, dee dubbedy, dubbedy dum-dum, dee dubbedy . . ."

She frowned. *What is that noise?* she wondered.

"Dubbedy dum-dum, dee dubbedy, dubbedy dum-dum, dee dubbedy . . ."

Daisy jumped off her seat, got down on her hands and knees, and peered beneath the chair. At first, all she could see were an old pen and a ball of fluff, but as she looked more closely, she saw a tiny ant sitting in the dust, moving his head back and forth to the rhythm of the song.

So I wasn't imagining things, Daisy thought.

"Dubbedy dum-dum, dee dubbedy, dubbedy dum-dum, dee dubbedy . . ."

"Hello there, little ant," she said. "That's a nice song you're singing."

"Aaaaaaheee!"

The ant jumped up into the air and slowly backed away toward the baseboard.

"Don't hurt me!" he said. "Don't step on me with those big shoes!"

Daisy leaned closer. "I'm not going to hurt you," she replied. "I was just enjoying your song."

The ant stopped.

"Really?" he asked. "You like my song?"

Daisy smiled.

"Yes, I do," she said.

"I made it up myself," said the ant proudly. "Guess what it's called."

"I don't know," replied Daisy. " 'Dubbedy Dum-Dum'?"

The ant was quiet for a moment.

"Lucky guess," he said at last.

Daisy sat back on her heels, stuck out her bottom lip, and blew so that her bangs puffed up in the air. Today was turning out to be just as strange as yesterday.

"I'm supposed to be down in the Big Room where they're dropping their cookies," the ant explained. "Cookies and sugar."

"The cafeteria, you mean?" asked Daisy.

"Yes," said the ant. "There were twenty of us in the patrol, you see. I was singing and dancing and enjoying myself and then the corporal said, 'Hey, Shorty, shuddup!' So then I sat down and started to cry. And when I looked up again, they were all gone."

"Poor you," said Daisy
sympathetically.

"Yes," replied the ant. "Poor me is right."

"Why was the corporal mad at you?"

"He says ants who sing get squashed by the big shoes.
So now I'm doing all my singing under the big chair. See?"

"I do see," said Daisy, trying
not to laugh. "Out of the way
of the big shoes, I guess?"

"Exactly," said the ant. "If you're
squished by the big shoes, you can't sing
anymore and that's bad and not happy. And," he added,
"I like being happy."

"Me too," agreed Daisy.

"You don't look happy," said the ant. "Are you scared
of the big shoes too?"

"No," said Daisy. "Big shoes don't really
bother me. It's just . . ." She took a deep
breath. "Yesterday I was talking to a dog,
and then I chatted with some gerbils,
and now I'm talking to an ant. And—I

don't mean to be rude—but it's all a bit weird. So now I'm beginning to wonder if I might be dreaming."

"Oh, no," said the ant. "If you were dreaming, you'd be snorking."

"Snorking?" Daisy asked. "What's that?"

"You know," said the ant. He lay down on his side, put two legs under his head, and made little puffing noises. "Snorking."

"Oh, *snoring,*" said Daisy. "Well, yes, I guess I would."

The ant scampered closer and looked up at her.

"Guess what?"

"What?"

"I'm not happy either."

"Oh, dear," whispered Daisy. "Why not?"

"I *told* you," wailed the ant. "I'm lost!"

"Lost?" said Daisy.

"Yes," said the ant. "Completerly and utterly."

"Well, maybe I can help," offered Daisy. "I know where the cafeteria is."

The ant shook his head. "No, no, I don't want cookies anymore. I'm tired. I want to go home."

"Oh," said Daisy. "Well, which way is your anthill?"

"If I knew that," replied the ant, "I wouldn't be lost, would I?"

"I guess not," agreed Daisy. "But how did you get here in the first place?"

"Marched," said the ant. "That's how ants get everywhere. Marchy-marchy-marchy, under the green wood-slab and over the brown shoe-field."

Daisy thought for a moment. "Oh, you mean the front entrance," she said, remembering the green double doors at the end of the corridor. She guessed that the shoe-field was probably the doormat where people wiped their feet. "I can take you there if you like. Climb up and I'll give you a lift."

Daisy stretched out her arm beneath the chair so that her hand was almost touching the ant. He took a few steps back and then slowly began to walk forward again.

"Don't squish me now," he said.

"Stop worrying," said Daisy. "I won't hurt you."

The ant touched the side of Daisy's finger with his tiny feelers and tickled his way along into the middle of her palm.

"Ready!" he said. "Off we go!"

"OK," said Daisy. "Hold on tight."

She was about to pull her hand from beneath the chair when she heard footsteps and looked up to see Mr. Blake, the principal, standing behind her.

"Ah, Daisy Dawson," he said. "What are you up to?"

Quick as a flash, Daisy folded her fingers over the top of the ant and jumped to her feet.

"Sorry, Mr. Blake," she said. "I've just come to deliver the attendance book."

"Hey!" called a little voice. "What's going on?"

"Shush!" said Daisy.

"I beg your pardon?" said Mr. Blake.

"Sorry," said Daisy. "I didn't mean you."

41

Mr. Blake glanced around.

"Then who did you mean, exactly?"

"Who's there?"

"No one," said Daisy.

"Young lady," said Mr. Blake, "do you make a habit of saying 'shush' to no one?"

"Is it your corporal?"

"Yes," said Daisy. "Kind of." She glanced up and saw that Mr. Blake was looking annoyed.

"I mean, no!" she added hurriedly. "No, I don't make a habit of saying 'shush' to no one." She wiped her forehead with the back of her hand. This was getting complicated.

"Well, then," said Mr. Blake, taking off his glasses and polishing them with a cloth. "Perhaps you would like to explain."

"*Daaaaai-zeeeee!* Can I go back to my hill now, please? I want to get to sleeping and snorking. Daisy, Daisy, *Daaaaai-zeeeee!*"

"Would you please shut *up* for a minute?"

said Daisy angrily. Then she looked up at Mr. Blake and blushed as she realized what she had just said.

Mr. Blake glared at her so fiercely that her knees went weak.

"*What* did you say?" he demanded.

"Oh no, no, no—I didn't mean *you,* Mr. Blake. I was, I was . . ."—Daisy thought desperately for a moment and was hit by a sudden flash of inspiration—"I was talking to my stomach!"

When he heard this, Mr. Blake passed a hand over his eyes and shook his head.

"Your stomach?" he repeated wearily.

"Yes, Mr. Blake. I don't think I had enough breakfast. It's been some morning."

"You're telling me."

Daisy tried to ignore the fact that the ant was now doing a very energetic and tickly jig around the palm of her hand. Instead, she did her best to look serious.

Mr. Blake sighed. "Daisy, I really don't know what's gotten into you today, but I suggest that whatever it is, you let it out again as soon as possible."

"Yes, Mr. Blake," said Daisy, trying hard not to giggle as the ant continued to boogie around inside her hand. "I'll definitely let it out as soon as I can."

Mr. Blake took off his glasses again and waved her away with the back of his hand. "Go on then. Back to your classroom."

"See ya, Blakey Boy!" called the ant. "Careful with those shoes!"

"You nearly got me in big trouble back there," said Daisy as she slipped out through the double doors onto the playground.

"Nothing to do with me," said the ant. "I was just dancing."

"Hmm," said Daisy. "And interrupting."

"Yes," said the ant. "Dancing and interrupting. I'm good at those things."

"Tell me something," said Daisy. "Don't you think it's strange that we're talking to each other?"

"Nope," said the ant. "I'll talk to anyone who's listening. Last week I talked to a caterpillar. That *was* strange."

"Why?" asked Daisy.

"Well, we were looking at the birds in the sky and he said, 'I'll be up there flying with them one day.' So I said, 'Yeah, right. Only if they eat you first!'"

"Actually, he was telling the truth," said Daisy. "Didn't you know? He'll turn into a butterfly next spring."

The ant laughed. "I like you," he said. "You're funny."

They reached the edge of the playground, and Daisy knelt down on the soft grass.

"There," she said. "Do you think you can find your way home now?"

"Oh, my house, my house!" cried the ant happily as Daisy opened her hand.

"I see my house!"

He walked to the end of Daisy's finger and stepped down onto a blade of grass. Then he turned around and waved his feelers at her.

"Thanks for the lift, Daisy! I'll be seeing you again some day!"

"I hope so," said Daisy. She watched him crawl down the green stem to the brown earth below. "But how will I know it's you?"

"Easy," replied the ant.

"I'll be the one who's singing!"

At that moment, a window opened and Daisy heard the familiar sound of Miss Frink's voice shouting at her from across the playground.

"Daisy Dawson," she yelled, "come back into the classroom this instant!"

"Uh-oh," said Daisy. "Got to go!"

But when she looked around, the ant had gone.

Daisy sat silently for a moment, breathing the scent of warm earth and listening to the murmur of the bees.

"Good-bye," she whispered. "Watch out for those shoes!"

Then she jumped up and ran across the playground, hopping carefully over a small line of ants before disappearing through the double doors into the cool shadows of the corridor.

Chapter 4
Sky-Flowers

As soon as school was over, Daisy

 burst out through the front doors

and ran as fast as she could up

the lane.

Leaning on the gate, she rested her chin on
the top and called, "Boom, where are you?"

When there was no reply, she cupped
her hands around her mouth and shouted,
"Boom, please! It's me—Daisy!"

"You're wasting your breath," said a husky voice beside her.

Daisy looked around to see a sleek gray cat staring up at her with cool green eyes.

"Boom's gone. Didn't you know?"

"But he can't be," said Daisy, who was already getting used to having conversations with animals. "I only spoke to him yesterday."

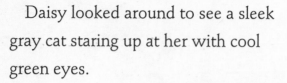

"Well yesterday was yesterday," replied the cat. "And today is today." It licked one of its paws, then looked up at Daisy again.

"The name's Trixie, by the way. Trixie McDixie if you want the whole of it, though there's not many that do."

She rubbed against the fence and padded closer.

"I warned him only the other day, but that dog always thinks he knows best. Well, not this time he doesn't."

"Trixie," said Daisy, "what are you talking about?"

"OK, listen up. Every morning at about eleven-thirty, Boom goes into town to see the butcher's boy. He shows up, does his whiny dog thing, and then the boy lobs a couple of scraggy bones at him. Can't see the attraction myself, but Boom says it's kind of a tradition, and he never misses it. Until now, that is."

"Why?" asked Daisy. "What happened?"

"There's a new dogcatcher in town. Word on the street is that any dog without a tag is getting picked up and thrown in the slammer. Boom just laughed when I told him about it. But he won't be laughing now. If no one claims him by the end of the week, they'll send him where they send all unwanted dogs."

"Where's that?" whispered Daisy.

"How should I know?" said Trixie. "All I know is that once a dog gets sent there, he never comes back."

"But that's terrible!" said Daisy. "We've got to do something!"

"Hmmm," purred Trixie. "Well, let's see. Do you know where he's being kept? No. Could you get him out of there if you did? Probably not. So are you going to waste my time discussing it with me? Let's hope not."

"You don't seem to care very much," said Daisy, getting cross.

"I'm a cat," said Trixie. "Cats don't do drama."

"So that's it, then?" asked Daisy. "You're just going to sit there and do nothing?"

"No," said Trixie calmly. "I'm going to say that if that silly dog had listened to me in the first place, he would never have gotten himself into this mess. Now if you'll excuse me," she added, strolling slowly toward the bushes, "I have a dinner date with a rabbit." And with that, she disappeared into the undergrowth.

The only sounds were a gentle breeze
rustling the leaves and, in the distance,
a sparrow singing songs about rain.

Daisy stared after Trixie, shocked that she
could be so unfeeling. Then she put her head
against the gate and started to cry, her tears
dripping down onto the cool green grass
below.

"Hush now, my dear," said a soft voice.
"Nothing's as bad as all that."

Daisy lifted her head to find herself
staring into the face of the white mare
who lived in the field.

"Oh," she said.
"Hello." She dried her
eyes with the back of
her hand and felt
the horse's

warm breath in her hair. "Who are you?"

"My name's Meadowsweet," said the mare. "And you must be Daisy Dawson."

"Yes," said Daisy, still sniffling. "How did you know?"

"A yellow butterfly told me," replied Meadowsweet. "She also told me that you helped her when she was in trouble. So now you should tell me why you're so sad, and maybe I can help you."

"I'm not the one who needs help," said Daisy sadly. "It's Boom."

"Boom?" replied Meadowsweet, sounding surprised. "Why, what's he been up to?"

"Do you know him?" asked Daisy.

Meadowsweet stamped her foot and whinnied loudly. "Boom's lived here ever since he was born," she explained. "He's always been so kind and thoughtful, even as a puppy. When I got frightened by fireworks one evening, he told me to just think of them as sky-flowers and he stayed up all night with me, making sure I was all right. I've never forgotten it. So what's happened?"

Daisy carefully recounted the story that Trixie had told her. When she finished, Meadowsweet leaned over the gate and put her head against Daisy's cheek, so that her warm breath tickled Daisy's ear.

"Don't you listen to that old sourpuss," she whinnied. "Whatever happens, you and I will find a way to bring Boom home again."

Chapter 5

Mission Impossible

"Dad," whispered Daisy when her father had covered her with the blanket and kissed her good night. "Do you believe that animals can talk?"

He stopped in the doorway and turned back to look at her.

"Of course," he said.

"Really?" asked Daisy.

"Yes, I'm sure they can—at least in their

own way. Otherwise, how would rabbits warn each other that a fox was coming? Or a bee tell its friends about a field full of flowers?"

"Oh," said Daisy. "I hadn't thought of that."

"Of course," her father went on, "the really interesting thing would be if we could understand what they were saying." He chuckled. "That would be something, wouldn't it?"

"Yes," Daisy whispered as he turned out the light. "It certainly would."

At first, Daisy wasn't sure what had woken her. The moonlight traced silver patterns across the floorboards, and as she rubbed her eyes, she heard a faint tap-tap-tapping at the window. Cautiously she pulled back the curtains and was surprised to see a little gray squirrel sitting on the ledge. It waved when it saw her and pointed at the window latch.

Daisy quickly opened the window, and
the squirrel jumped down onto her bed.

"Greetings," it said in a small, elegant
voice. "I am here on a top-secret mission."
It beckoned her closer, put a paw up to its
mouth, and whispered, "No one must ever
know of my existence."

"How exciting," said Daisy, trying to look
serious. "Are you a spy?"

"Maybe I am," replied the squirrel, "and
maybe I'm not."

He looked slowly left and right as if checking that no one was listening, and then whispered, "The blue donkey . . . is under the mattress."

Daisy leaned over the side of her bed and peered beneath it. "Really?" she asked. "Are you sure?"

"No, no, no, *no!*" replied the squirrel, exasperation creeping into his voice. He cupped both paws around his mouth and said again in a loud whisper, "THE BLUE DONKEY IS UNDER THE MATTRESS!"

Daisy shook her head. "I'm sorry, but I don't have the faintest idea what you're talking about."

He dropped his paws and sighed heavily.

"It's secret code!" he explained. "Trouble is, I'm the only one who understands it."

"Never mind," said Daisy brightly. "How about you tell me in ordinary language?"

"OK," he said. "We've found Boom. We know where he is."

"Oh," gasped Daisy, picking him up and kissing him on the tip of the nose. "That's wonderful news, Mr. Squirrel!"

"Oh, well now, it was nothing really. I—I—please, call me Cyril," he said, blushing in a way that only squirrels can.

"It's nice to meet you, Cyril," said Daisy, placing him gently back down onto the blanket. "So tell me," she went on, "where did you find Boom?"

"Well, that's the problem," said Cyril. "At the moment he's locked up in a temporary kennel on the outskirts of town, run by some crazy lady, apparently. But they're going to move him to the big-city kennel in the morning. And once they've done that, we won't have a hope of rescuing him." Cyril's voice dropped. "We have to get him out *tonight*."

"Tonight?" whispered Daisy excitedly. "But how?"

"Well," said the squirrel, eyeing Daisy's pajamas disdainfully, "getting dressed would be a start."

A few minutes later, Daisy clicked the front door shut behind her and followed Cyril down the driveway. As they turned the corner, she saw Meadowsweet waiting beneath a streetlamp.

"Good job, Cyril," said the old mare, bending her head down toward Daisy. "Climb aboard, Daisy. We have to move quickly."

Daisy clambered up onto Meadowsweet's
back, the moon shining silver above the
chimneys. Cyril scrambled up onto her
shoulder and then they were off, the squirrel
calling out directions as they galloped away
across moonlit fields, the cool night air
blowing softly in their faces.

After about twenty minutes, they came to a white farmhouse on the edge of a forest. Behind it was a high wooden fence with a sign that said:

```
KRACKDOWN KENNELS
     KEEP OUT
```

"Are you sure this is it?" asked Daisy.

"Absolutely," said Cyril. "I got a couple of pigeons and some mice to case the joint this afternoon. Cost me a few acorns, but if you want good information, you've got to pay for it these days."

"We think Boom's the only one in there at the moment," explained Meadowsweet. "The other dogs were moved out last week."

"OK," said Cyril, perching on Meadowsweet's head. "Here's the plan. On the other side of that fence is a row of metal cages. Boom's in cage number seven. But the cages are locked, and the keys are kept by the fierce old bat who owns the place."

"Where does she keep them?" asked Daisy.

"On her bedside table," replied Cyril.

Daisy chewed her lip. "That's not so good."

"Ah, but that's where you come in," he explained. "I get in through the cat flap and unlatch the door, you come upstairs and open the bedroom door for me, and I sneak in and swipe the keys. We'll be in and out before she's even got time to grab her baseball bat."

"Baseball bat?" repeated Daisy nervously. "Did you say 'baseball bat'?"

"Don't worry," said Cyril. "She couldn't hit a home run if you pitched her a watermelon."

Daisy took a deep breath.
"OK, then. I guess we'd better
get on with it."

"That's the spirit," said
Cyril, leaping up onto the fence.
"Who dares wins!"

As he disappeared over the top,
Daisy stood on Meadowsweet's
back, hooked her fingers over the
fence, and pulled herself up. She
jumped down, nearly squashing
Cyril flat. He
rolled out of
the way just in
time. "Hey!" he
squeaked. "I'm on
your side,
remember?"

The house was in darkness as they approached, and Cyril slipped quietly through the cat flap. A few seconds later, he reappeared with a key in his mouth and Daisy quickly opened the front door.

Standing in the darkness at the bottom of the stairs, she felt her fingers tingle with a mixture of excitement and fear.

"Come on," said Cyril, scampering upstairs toward the bedroom.

The house smelled of old carpets and decaying flowers. Daisy stopped and held her breath every time a stair creaked, but at last she reached the bedroom door, where Cyril was tapping his foot and beckoning impatiently to her.

"This is it," he whispered. "You open the door, I'll grab the keys, and then—*whoosh!*—we're *out* of here."

"OK," Daisy whispered back. "But be careful."

She twisted the doorknob, and the door creaked open. Over on the bed, a large mound rose and fell beneath the covers, accompanied by loud snores and wheezes.

"Look," said Cyril. "What d'you figure?"

Daisy followed his gaze to the bedside table and, trying to ignore the baseball bat propped up against it, saw a small lamp, a glass of water, and a bunch of keys.

"Bingo," she whispered. "Go for it, Cyril!"

Cyril ran around the end of the bed and jumped neatly up onto the table.

Unfortunately for him, the tabletop had
been waxed and polished that very morning,
and now it was as slippery as an ice rink.
Daisy saw the look of horror on his face as
he pirouetted unsteadily across the surface
before colliding with the table lamp
and knocking the glass to the floor
with a crash.

For a few short
moments, time seemed to stand still.
Then a large, red-faced woman rose up from
the covers and began to scream so loudly
that Daisy jumped backward and bumped
her head against the doorframe.

"It's a rat!" screeched the woman, pointing
a thick, stubby finger at Cyril as he stood
transfixed amid the wreckage of the tabletop.
"I'm being attacked by a filthy rat!"

As she sprang out of bed with a heavy
thud, Cyril came to his senses and shot out

of the bedroom like a
stone from a catapult.

"Run, Daisy!" he squeaked,
rocketing past. "She's after us!"

Daisy turned and began leaping down the
stairs three at a time.

"Did you hear that?" yelled Cyril as they
burst through the back door and ran toward
the kennels. "She called me a *rat*!"

"Never mind that," said Daisy. They
skidded to a halt in front of cage number
seven. "Where are the keys?"

Cyril looked at her awkwardly.

"I—I . . . might have, er, dropped them at
the top of the stairs," he said. "I sort of . . .
didn't want to get clobbered."

"Great," said Daisy.

They looked around to see the kennel owner standing at the back door, brandishing the baseball bat. "Where are you, you sneaky rat?" she shrieked. "Come on out or I'll whack you with my bat!"

"Quick, Cyril," urged Daisy, crouching next to the cages. "What's Plan B?" She put her hand against the wire of the cage to steady herself, but the door swung open and she fell forward onto her hands and knees.

"Cyril!" she whispered. "Look, it's open!" Cyril squeaked in surprise and disappeared into the cage. Daisy glanced back to see the large figure of the kennel owner walking slowly across the grass toward them, clutching the baseball bat firmly in her right hand.

"Cyril," Daisy called nervously, "she's coming!"

The squirrel emerged from the gloom shaking his head. "This is not going as planned," he whispered. "There's no sign of him."

"Hey, you there!" shouted the woman. "Girl with the rat!"

Cyril looked up at Daisy with a pained expression.

"What *is* it with this rat thing?" he asked.

"Cyril," said Daisy, "she looks pretty angry. What are we going to do?"

Cyril watched calmly as the woman stomped toward them. "Emergency tactics," he said. "I'll create a diversion, and you make a break for it over the fence."

"But she might whack you," Daisy protested, cowering back against the cage. "With her bat!"

"You forget," said Cyril loftily, "that she is a mere civilian, whereas *I* am a highly trained squirrel operative. The poor woman doesn't stand a *chance*." And before Daisy had time to answer, he ran off at top speed across the grass.

There was a sudden swishing noise and Cyril leaped high into the air with a cry of "Hiiiiii-*yah*!", holding his paws like a tiny ninja warrior as the baseball bat swept harmlessly beneath him. Eyes narrowed, he made small, high-pitched squeaks, jumping deftly out of the way as the hapless kennel owner took more swipes at him. "Go, Daisy!" he shouted. "Run for it!"

But as Daisy reached the fence, a booming voice stopped her in her tracks.

"And where do you think you're going?" The red-faced woman was marching straight toward her. "You stay right where you are, young lady!"

Stretching up on tiptoe, Daisy tried desperately to reach the top of the fence, but it was too high. Her fingers scrabbled uselessly against the wood as two strong hands grabbed her arms.

"Ha-*ha*!" cried the woman triumphantly. "Now I've got you."

Shaking with fear, Daisy leaned her forehead against the fence and called, "Meadowsweet, help me, please!"

The next
moment there
was a thundering
of hooves, and
Meadowsweet sailed
over the fence to land
beside Daisy with an earth-
shaking thump. The woman's
mouth fell open in amazement, and she
sank to the ground with her hands clamped
firmly over her eyes.

"It's a bad dream, Beatrice," she mumbled to herself, shaking her head and rubbing her eyes. "You're having a bad dream, that's all. Dancing rats and flying horses! Just count to ten and it'll all be over. One, two . . ."

Meadowsweet tossed her mane, called, "Climb aboard, brave soldiers," and before Daisy knew it, they had leaped back over the fence and were galloping away through silent woods and moonlit fields toward home.

*   *   *

As Daisy opened the gate to let Meadowsweet into her field, she saw that Cyril looked sad and angry with himself.

"Mission most definitely *not* accomplished," he said miserably. "Now we'll never see Boom again."

"It's not your fault, Cyril," said Daisy. "You did everything you could."

"But it wasn't enough." Cyril cried bitterly. "It wasn't *enough*!"

"Oh puh-*lease*," said a sharp voice from somewhere in the shadows. "I've already had enough of that dog whining all night. Don't make me listen to the squirrel as well."

Peering into the darkness, Daisy could see the green eyes of Trixie McDixie staring at them from beneath the horse trough.

"For your information," replied Cyril icily, "*that dog,* as you call him, has been taken away from us forever. But I don't suppose you care about that, do you? I bet you're not even the slightest bit worried."

"You're right," said Trixie, carelessly licking her paw with her little pink tongue. "I'm not worried at all."

"Trixie!" Meadowsweet scolded. "You should be ashamed of yourself."

The cat stopped for a moment and twitched her whiskers in surprise.

"Oh," she said. "You think so?" Then she padded out from beneath the horse trough and called huskily, "What about you, Boom? Do you think I should be ashamed of myself?"

Cyril frowned and looked at Daisy.

Daisy looked at Meadowsweet.

All three of them stared at the old barn.

Slowly, a large bloodhound emerged with the somewhat bewildered look of a dog

who is still half asleep. Daisy flung her arms
around his neck and cried, "Oh, Boom,
you're safe, you're safe!"

"Well, *duh*!" said Trixie.

Meadowsweet stamped and whinnied
with joy, but Cyril was flummoxed.

"I don't get it," he said. "The mice told me
the keys were in the bedroom. I even picked
them up. So how did Boom escape?"

"That," replied Trixie disdainfully, "is the trouble with mice. They may taste good, but they know nothing about modern security systems."

She pushed a small rectangle of plastic toward Cyril, who sniffed it and shrugged. "What's this?"

"This, my friend, is the key to the new electronic locks the kennel owner had fitted last week. The old keys you picked up were completely useless. I got chatting with the tomcat who lives there, and he told me about this swipe card that opens all the cages. So while the owner was out shopping this afternoon, I slipped in through the cat flap, took the card off the table, and gave the silly dog his freedom back."

"But how did you get him over the fence?" asked Cyril.

"No need," said Trixie. "Royston Rabbit owed me a favor or two, so after dinner last night I got him and his boys to dig a hole around the back. Nothing fancy, of course — just big enough to let an old hound squeeze through."

Cyril stared at Trixie for a long time and then shook his head in disbelief.

"Do you mean to tell me," he said, "that while we were out there *risking our lives* this evening, you and Boom were back here relaxing?"

"Well, I wouldn't exactly call it relaxing," replied Trixie. "That dog snores like a sick horse."

Screwing his paws up into angry little fists, Cyril jumped up and down and squeaked, "Why on EARTH didn't you tell us before?"

Trixie shrugged. "Because, my dear squirrel, you never asked."

Cyril stamped his foot, scowled furiously, and scampered up a nearby tree trunk in a major huff.

"Well," said Meadowsweet as Daisy hugged Boom and Cyril sat sulking on a branch of the old oak, "I have to say, Trixie, you certainly showed us the way to do it this time."

Trixie stared coolly at Meadowsweet for a long moment, her eyes glowing green in the moonlight.

"So what's new?" she purred.

And with that, she turned her back and slunk off into the shadows.

Chapter 6
Daisy's Magic

"Now, Daisy," called her mother as Daisy danced down the garden path and swung around the gatepost, "don't dawdle, and don't be late!"

The sun shone brightly from a cloudless sky, and somewhere among the green leaves, a blackbird sang a song about buttercups and rainbows.

"Don't worry, Mom," Daisy called back over her shoulder. "Daisy Dawson is on her way!"

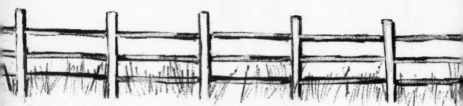

She looked at her watch and saw that
there was still plenty of time before school
started. The family had spent the weekend
away staying with her grandparents, and
now Daisy was excited to see Boom again
and show him what she'd gotten for him.

She crossed the road carefully and ran up
the path toward the field where she found
Meadowsweet grazing peacefully in the
morning sun.

"Hello, Meadowsweet!" said Daisy
happily. "Where is everyone this morning?"

Meadowsweet shook her head and
snorted. Then she bent down and began
tugging at the grass again.

"Hey, Meadowsweet," said Daisy. "Aren't
you talking to me today?"

"She ain't called Meadowsweet," said
a voice behind her. "She's called Dobbin."

Daisy turned around to see the farmer
coming up the lane. "Reckon you should be
in school learning something useful, young
'un," he said as he passed. "Not wastin' your
time talkin' to dumb animals."

As Daisy watched the grumpy old farmer
walk away up the path, she suddenly felt
completely alone, as though the ground had
opened up and swallowed everything she'd
ever believed in.

It's time to wake up . . . whispered the voice in her head. *They were only dreams . . . None of it was real . . . They were only dreams. . . .*

In the silence that followed, Daisy blinked back tears and felt her happiness evaporate like morning mist. For the first time in her life, she began to suspect that the things people said about her were true. That she spent too much time living in imaginary worlds that didn't really exist. Suddenly it was obvious to her, as clear as the sunlight that shone through the trees.

Her adventures with the animals had been dreams—nothing more. Meadowsweet was just a horse called Dobbin, and everyone knew that horses couldn't talk.

And so, as Daisy began to wander back along the path toward school, she decided that the time had come to stop believing in her dreams. It was time to grow up and join the real world.

From now on, she would listen.

She would be good.

She would be on time. . . .

"Hey, my dear," called a familiar voice.
"Going so soon?"

Daisy stopped and frowned. Then she
shook her head and began walking again.

Stop it, she told herself. *Grow up!*

"Daisy, my love!" called the voice
behind her. "Where are you going?"

Daisy turned and saw that the white mare was leaning over the gate, staring at her.

"Meadowsweet?" she asked, hardly daring to hope.

The mare nodded. "Yes, of course, dear. Who did you think it was?"

Daisy was confused. "But . . . when I spoke to you just now . . . you didn't answer."

"Well, of course not, my lovely," replied Meadowsweet. "I could hardly have a chat with you while that silly old farmer was standing there, could I? *Dobbin,* indeed!"

Daisy suddenly felt as though her heart were going to burst. She ran back up the

path, flung her arms around Meadowsweet's
nose, and kissed her.

"Well, now," said Meadowsweet, her
breath warm in Daisy's ear. "That's more
like my Daisy."

Then she glanced over
Daisy's shoulder and said,
"Look. There's someone
else to see you."

When Daisy turned around, she saw that Boom was sitting in the lane, gazing up at her with his serious brown eyes.

"Boom!" she cried.

"Hello, Daisy," he said in a voice that was deep and slow and kind. "I woke up early this morning and thought, *I wonder if my favorite little girl would like some company on her way to school*?"

Daisy smiled and thought that she had never been so happy in all her life.

"That would be wonderful," she said. "But before we go, I have something for you."

"For me?" asked Boom. Then after a moment's thought, he added, "Has it got ham in it?"

"No," said Daisy, reaching into her backpack, "but I think you'll like it anyway." She pulled out a small tag on a silver chain and held it up for Boom to see.

"What is it?" he asked.

"It's a name tag," said Daisy, kneeling down and fastening the chain around his neck. "It's got your name on the front and my name and telephone number on the back. If the dogcatcher ever sees you again, he'll think you belong to me and he'll leave you alone."

Boom looked up at Daisy.

"Do I?" he asked shyly.

"Do you what, Boom?"

"Do I belong to you?"

Daisy put her arms around him.

"Friends belong to one another," she said.
"Isn't that right, Meadowsweet?"

Meadowsweet nodded. "It's the best sort
of belonging there is."

Boom rested his chin contentedly in
Daisy's lap and for a few moments all was
silent except for the gentle humming of the
bees. Then suddenly he pricked up his ears
and barked twice.

"What is it, Boom?" Daisy asked, stroking
his head. "What's the matter?"

"Oh, nothing. I just think we should be
going, that's all."

"But why?" asked Daisy.

"Because," said Boom, "the school bell is ringing."

"Uh-oh," said Daisy. "I'm going to be late again, aren't I?" She stuck her bottom lip out and blew so that her bangs puffed up in the air. "Meadowsweet, do you mind if I ask you something before I go?"

"Not at all," said Meadowsweet. "Ask me anything."

"Do you think I'll always be able to talk to you all? Or do you think it's some kind of magic that might disappear one day?"

"I don't know," said Meadowsweet gently. "But what I do know is that whenever we talk, the magic seems to come from inside of you. It's part of who you are, Daisy Dawson, and that is a very rare thing. You must always look after it, and keep it close to your heart."

"Thank you, Meadowsweet," said Daisy, kissing the old mare lightly on the nose. "I'll try."

Then she hitched up her backpack and ran away down the hot, dusty lane toward the gates of Nettlegreen Elementary School, with her best friend, Boom, by her side.